MAGICAL CHRONICLES

Edited By Lynsey Evans

First published in Great Britain in 2024 by:

Young Writers
Remus House
Coltsfoot Drive
Peterborough
PE2 9BF
Telephone: 01733 890066
Website: www.youngwriters.co.uk

FOREWORD

Welcome Reader!

Are you ready to discover weird and wonderful creatures that you'd never even dreamed of?

For Young Writers' latest competition we asked primary school pupils to create a creature of their own invention, and then write a mini saga about it - a hard task! However, they rose to the challenge magnificently and the result is this fantastic collection full of creepy critters and bizarre beasts!

Here at Young Writers our aim is to encourage creativity in children and to inspire a love of the written word, so it's great to get such an amazing response, with some absolutely fantastic stories.

Not only have these young authors created imaginative and inventive creatures, they've also crafted wonderful tales to showcase their creations. These stories are brimming with inspiration and cover a wide range of themes and emotions - from fun to fear and back again!

I'd like to congratulate all the young authors in this anthology, I hope this inspires them to continue with their creative writing.

CONTENTS

Ethan Wilkinson (11)	53
Dylan Tailor (11)	54
Lucas Dowdall-Branston (11)	55
Layla Sutton (11)	56
Sebastian Springthorpe (11)	57
Esmé Endacott (10)	58
Luca Smart	59
Sienna Sandhu (11)	60
Millie Morris (11)	61
Kian Norton (10)	62
Phoebe McKinlay (10)	63
Lucia Alonzi (11)	64
Ruth Brown (10)	65
Sofia Hanmer (11)	66
Freddie Lines (11)	67
George Harrison (10)	68
Toby Suart (10)	69
Leo Marlow (11)	70
Aura Williams (10)	71
Elizabeth Brunt (11)	72
Mila Higginson (10)	73
Freya Sharpe (11)	74
Seb Seed	75
Jacob Sullinskozicki (11)	76
Macie Bentley (11)	77
Lottie Pritchard (11)	78
Anaya Joshi (11)	79
Shayan Mashru (11)	80
Arthur Warner (11)	81
Filip Jasinski (11)	82

Springfield Community Primary School, Burnley

Lola Clark (10)	83
Abigail Warren (9)	84
Aarav Kataria (10)	85
Adam Ahmed (10)	86
Hallie Noone (9)	87
Maisy Davison (9)	88
Jonathan Varela (10)	89
Zuha Daud (10)	90
Zaineb Muhammad (10)	91
Saffa Sadiq (10)	92

Teodora Georgieva (10)	93
Willson Crowther (10)	94
Nikola Kotsev (9)	95
Connie Ellerton (10)	96
Kelly Peek (10)	97

St George's (VC) CE Primary School & Nursery, Kidderminster

Talitha Mtawali (11)	98
Ezza Anwar Anwar (9)	99
Tiarna Walker (8)	100
Syeda Sadiqa Ahmed (10)	101
Aleema Begum (10)	102
Sameera Khatun (8)	103
Chase Alexander Reeves (7)	104
Zakiya Ahmed (8)	105
Katlyn Hussey (10)	106
Junior (Steven) Hussey (9)	107
Maicey Tilling (11)	108
Anureet Kaur (8)	109
Timur Turan (8)	110

Stow On The Wold Primary School, Stow On The Wold

Alex Cripps (10)	111
Mollie Tustin (10)	112
Bethany Antiojo (10)	113
Harrison Jones (10)	114
Ella Goode (11)	115
Lily O'Kane (11)	116
Gracie Adams (10)	117
Eric Rothera (10)	118
Kush Kennedy (10)	119
Elijah Rogers (9)	120
Annabelle Wright (9)	121
Jude Williams (9)	122
Thea Shaw (11)	123

The Oratory Preparatory School, Goring Heath

Wilbury Primary School, Edmonton

THE STORIES

Bubbles The Life-Saver

Finally, the moment everyone was waiting for. Bubbles was deployed - he zoomed through the water, steering with his majestic purple mohawk. He arrived, but the casualty was drowning fast. Could he save their life? He blew the biggest bubble he could! The suspense built up... the person floated to the surface and started breathing. He was saved. Suddenly, another person was drowning, but mighty Bubbles zoomed to the rescue of the near-death casualty and another great success! Proudly, Bubbles swam back home after his first day on the job.
When he got back, everyone exclaimed rewardingly, "Well done, Bubbles!"

George Grice (11)
Great Massingham CE Primary School, Great Massingham

Crazy Creatures Of Japan

On the 10th of April 1912, the crazy creatures went around Japan, where they lived. People were out shopping and playing games. In Tokoyo, people were eating sushi at restaurants and enjoying themselves. Some crazy creatures went to the cinema and watched movies about Japan. Meanwhile, in Belfast, Ireland, they had just built a ship called the Titanic. Back in Japan, people were screaming in fright. They had just been warned that there was a tsunami coming, but when everyone was saying goodbye to the future, a loud honk sound was heard. Steaming to the rescue was the RMS Titanic.

George Ridgwell (8)
Great Massingham CE Primary School, Great Massingham

Saving Glowshroom

Spikeypops held his breath. An image of the barren wasteland covered in ashes and devouring fires flooded his head. Thorntail, his enemy, had burned it to make room for his fire machine but was denied planning permission. He tiptoed past the guards; he needed to get that acorn to revive the springs! Once the guards were out of sight, he sprinted to the first trap room, the Stone Jumps. Spikeypops leapt from stone to stone and completed the course. Finally, he needed to pass the lasers. Ducking and diving, he grabbed the acorn from the pedestal. Glowshroom Springs was saved.

Florence Doherty (11)
Great Massingham CE Primary School, Great Massingham

3

Bob And Warlar's Adventure

One sunny day, Bob found a volcano surrounded by a lake. There was also a hut. Bob walked in and inside was a half-water half-lava man.

The creature, Warlar, said, "Hi, come in, here's a snack and a drink."

They discussed their lives. Bob found out that Warlar was travelling to different planets to find out new things about them. Warlar asked for Bob's help. Bob listed some new unexplored planets. They gave each other some presents. Warlar was ready to go and visit those planets. They said their goodbyes. Everyone lived happily ever after.

Oliver Iles (8)

Great Massingham CE Primary School, Great Massingham

Treeso The Tree Monster

There once was a tree monster. He lived in the depths of the rainforest. He stayed asleep nearly his whole life, but was woken up by the loud sound of banging. It was a lumberjack. He was chopping down trees like mad. When the lumberjack wasn't looking, Treeso secretly ran away to the part of the rainforest where the tree-loving tribe lived. The tree-loving tribe looked at Treeso for a second. They didn't recognise him, but they didn't realise he was a new tree. Treeso was very happy with where he'd moved to. No lumberjack ever came again.

Dexter (7)
Great Massingham CE Primary School, Great Massingham

Shrimpy And Malum An Evil Apple

On Planet Doalot, a bored alien called Shrimpy sat in his seaweed bed reading, when all of a sudden, a loud bang sounded and a picture of an apple appeared in the sky. Suddenly, Shrimpy appeared, not in his bedroom, but in a room full of apples, with arms, legs and faces. Without a warning, they all started chanting one word, Malum. They made a path for a bigger apple. Shrimpy guessed that this was Malum, so he got ready to fight. Luckily, he started to get hungry and ate Malum. He called his friends and together, they finished Malum.

Henry Lockwood (10)
Great Massingham CE Primary School, Great Massingham

Slime Boy

Once upon a time in Slime Town, there was a little hero called Slime Boy.
One day, as Slime Boy was strolling around, he spotted a train stuck on the tracks. Curiously, Slime Boy approached the train and asked the passengers what had happened. They explained that the train was jammed. Without hesitating, Slime Boy knew he had to help. With his slimy body, he jumped onto the tracks and started pushing the train. Slowly but surely, the train began to move again. The passengers cheered with joy as Slime Boy saved the day once more.

Noah Anderson (10)
Great Massingham CE Primary School, Great Massingham

Mia Made Some New Friends

Mia went on an aeroplane to Florida. When she was there, she tried some new foods. First, she had some ice cream and said it was yummy. Second, she tried pizza, which was yucky. Next, she tried delicious chocolate. Then, she went to the park and made two new friends. They were called Holly and Poppy. Holly came to the swimming pool, and so did Poppy. It was Poppy's birthday, so she invited Mia and Holly to her party. Mia and Holly went to make a cake for Poppy. It was chocolate cake and Poppy was happy. Mia had made more friends.

Ava Carlton (7)

Great Massingham CE Primary School, Great Massingham

Luna The Kindness Creature

A girl from Earth was getting bullied, and Luna heard, so she set off to Earth from Birdeham. When Luna arrived, she went straight to the girl's school. The girl was in tears on a bench in the playground. Luna quickly shape-shifted into a plant so the girl would not see her. Luna took out a truth potion, turned invisible and went into the school. Luna went to the bully's classroom and tipped the potion into his drink bottle. When the boy drank his drink, he was kind and apologised to the girl who was crying on the bench.

Bethany Hurst (9)
Great Massingham CE Primary School, Great Massingham

Mechanical Bill

Once upon a time, a cute little monster called Mechanical Bill, was at school. He had a maths test. He was meant to be studying, but spent most of his time out of school fixing cars and rockets, on Planet Mechanical. He knew he was going to fail. But he took the test. The next day he saw his results. He got fifteen out of fifteen. Now he was happy. He could tell his family that he got fifteen out of fifteen. He started to do some fixing on the mighty rocket. That's what he liked doing best. Fixing mighty rockets and cars.

Freddie Harrison (9)

Great Massingham CE Primary School, Great Massingham

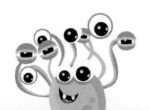

Untitled

In Egypt, it was a scorching hot day, and at the Pyramid of Giza, it was very windy and sand was blowing everywhere. All of a sudden, a body underneath the pyramid blasted out, and Pyramido appeared with one eye wide open. He called for his mum, "Mum?" but she was nowhere to be seen. Wiping the tears from his eyes, he went in search of a drink. He found the biggest lake; he was flabbergasted! Suddenly, as Pyramido stood drinking the fresh water, he saw a reflection. "Mum, it's you!" shouted Pyramido.

Cabe Gibbs (9)
Great Massingham CE Primary School, Great Massingham

Skate Or Scoot?

Zak, a crazy creature, was practising scooter-riding for a freestyle competition he'd seen last week. He was practising so hard but he realised he needed pads, so he went home and bought some new pads. But after he had to go for dinner. The next day, he got up really early to practise. The day had come, so he had breakfast and went in his mum's car. He had gone to compete. He pulled off loads of sick tricks. He even did five tail whips in one! It was insane! He ended up winning first place in the end.

Ralph Grice (9)
Great Massingham CE Primary School, Great Massingham

Fire Eyes

There was a young creature called Fire Eyes, and he lived in the forest. At school, he didn't have many friends; you see, he wasn't that kind of creature. He was the odd one out because he had five eyes. But one day, he had an idea. He would make friends, like, actually make a friend. He got to work; he worked day and night until *boom*! It exploded! Uh-oh, he was in trouble with the headteacher. He was worried, so he opened the door and ran back home, and the headteacher did follow him home.

Theo Carlton (8)
Great Massingham CE Primary School, Great Massingham

The Bubble Monster

It all began when someone was drowning in a river and the Bubble Monster blew a massive bubble. The human then started to float up in the air with a giant bubble force field around them, and they were saved.

Timmy Howlett (11)
Great Massingham CE Primary School, Great Massingham

The Origin Of Abiba

Despite the creature's unsettling appearance, she was usually left out when with others. But nobody knew her true appearance, as they believed she was a skinwalker. The most people had seen of her were her footprints. Although, it was believed she was unable to see due to her gouged-out eyes. The ears perched onto her head dripped blood. But since she usually skinwalked as a cat rumours said that she had cat ears instead of horns. The name Abiba was believed to mean death. Her father named her that because she was known to cause destruction and even death.

Mila Amir (10)
Heatherbrook Primary Academy, Beaumont Leys

Slimy Saves The World

Long ago, there were two brothers named Slimy and Sticky Mess. They didn't get on very well and decided to separate from each other.

A few years later, Sticky Mess got sent to prison for destroying the town. Slimey saved the day but celebrating was over when Sticky Mess broke out of jail, and it was up to Slimy to save the day. Sticky Mess was creating a mess and destroying the town, but just as all hope was gone, Slimy came to save the day. Everyone was celebrating and cheering for Slimy. He had saved the world!

Lola Ameer-Beg (10)

Heatherbrook Primary Academy, Beaumont Leys

Razzle's Redemption: A Laughter-Fuelled Revolution

In Hazbin Hotel's vibrant chaos, Razzle, a mischievous imp, conjured spells, blending laughter with redemption. His pranks, colourful disruptions, catalysed unexpected self-discovery, transforming despair into whimsical epiphanies.

One day, Razzle orchestrated a spell-binding comedy show, entwining dark humour with profound revelations. Initially sceptical, the audience found themselves laughing at their own flaws. Through laughter, Razzle uncovered dormant seeds of change, leaving an indelible mark on the souls of the damned.

Amidst the tumultuous turmoil, Razzle's unique mix of mischief and insight ignited a revolution of self-awareness, captivating judges and etching a profound place in everyone's hearts. Joy supremely reigns triumphant.

Roxy Gallett (10)
Hollywood Primary School, Hollywood

Another World

Many generations ago, when cats could fly, and trees could cry, Earth was a bizarre yet unique place. Back then, this planet was filled with various creatures, but on this Earth, in Asia, a particular girl was always intrigued by Earth's wonders. So, at dawn one day, she set off for an errand to explore more. While she was on her journey, a frenzied creature appeared before her.

"Oh my!"

"Hello there," said Edgar.

"You are...?"

"Spike, from Mars."

"By the way, my name is Charlotte. Genuinely sorry but I am running late for a meeting. Bye for now!"

"Wait!"

Hari Sanjeeviragjan (10)
Hollywood Primary School, Hollywood

The Friend

Not so long ago, there was a creature called O. O was a friendly, caring alien, but people judged him by his looks. O went to his dream destination, Earth. "I can't wait to make friends," said O in excitement. The next day something bad happened.

"O you don't belong here," Bug the Tron laughed. Then O ran out crying his heart out, but O met Eillieana.

"Hi, I am Ellieana, what's your name?" said Ellieana. "What's the matter?" said Ellieana.

"Oh, I am O. Wanna be friends?" O said.

"Yes," said Ellieana.

Molly Edwards (10)
Hollywood Primary School, Hollywood

The Disgusting Howler

After a long, deep sleep, the Disgusting Howler woke to find one of his teeth missing. He wasn't happy. He knew the tooth fairy had been. "Why didn't she wake me?" he disgustingly howled. Turning over his slimy, disgusting pillow, he found money! He wanted the tooth fairy to take all of his teeth to earn money. He thought, *if I could pay the King of Disgusting Howlers, I would not be disgusting anymore.* The King of Disgusting Howlers was paid in full. Howler now, no longer disgusting, works with the tooth fairies, wishing every child a good night's sleep.

Holly Jackson (10)

Hollywood Primary School, Hollywood

Planet Zog

Once upon a time, there was a minuscule, cream creature called Catich. Catich, the ruler of planet Zog, saw all the creatures, which were cyan lizards, luscious blood-like, red-coloured, fire-breathing dragons and glow-in-the-dark owls.

One day a gang called the Gamers Perils came to attack but everyone on planet Zog didn't want to besides the crazy fire-breathing dragons, but the Gamers Perils didn't care so they started to attack. In the blink of an eye, the fire-breathing dragons demolished the ice dragons from the Gamers Perils.

Harry Bourne (10)

Hollywood Primary School, Hollywood

Hairy Henry Saves The Day

The scary-looking sea monster can't make friends because everyone is scared of him. He sees an injured mermaid and offers to heal her with his magic hands. She says no and rushes away. He follows and asks again. Henry's big heart shrinks with sadness when she hides. He then finds the mermaid sleeping behind a rock and places his magic hand on her heart. She wakes up in shock and full of joy with no pain. She apologises to him and asks if they can become friends. He instantly says yes and grins. His big heart grows with happiness.

Keira Jeffrey (10)

Hollywood Primary School, Hollywood

Untitled

One day on Cube Land, a Volcanic Cube and Kevin Cube went to the Comet Cube and saw his enemy, Volcanic Blast. He was stealing buildings.

"We have to stop him," said Kevin Cube.

"Yeah, I know, but how? He is the strongest supervillain in the universe!"

"We have to gather a team of heroes."

Two months later, they had gathered a full squad of superheroes, travelling to Planet Squish.

"We're here!"

"Time to get our buildings back."

"*Charge! Arghh!*"

The greatest battle ever to be written.

"That was a good story, Grandad, goodnight."

Aadyn Walsh (10)
Parkhill Primary School, Leven

The Helper

Suddenly, a man needed my help. I asked, "What is wrong?"

"I have been hurt by a villain! He broke my leg!"

"Okay, let me see what I can do!"

"Argh! He has just struck a laser. It is coming right for us!"

"We don't need to worry, though, because I have my laser-proof metal suit. Let's get you sorted." I explained. "Now you should be able to walk."

"Yes, I can walk! Now can we get out of here?"

"Yeah, hold on."

"Yes, I hate that villain."

"How did that happen?"

"Well, we used to be friends."

Nathan Berry (10)
Parkhill Primary School, Leven

Miah's Crazy Imagination

Miah, bored like always, thought, *why would I have to know what fractions are? I'm never sharing.* Her teacher shouted, "Miah!" waving her hand. Shaking, she snapped back into reality. She was daydreaming. She was dreaming of a laser-shooting monster, Cyclamsy. Taking a moment, she realised her imagination was becoming reality as her monster rose from the ground. The teacher collapsed in shock. Miah had a lightbulb moment. Watching Cyclamsy appear from behind her teacher was thrilling. So many ideas were running through her head.

What could the monster do? How can this benefit Miah? All these ideas, until...

Miah Sam (11)
Parkhill Primary School, Leven

Untitled

One frosty evening, Tigeraffe was born. But he did not look like a normal animal. He was a rare, multianimal. Tigeraffe was from Creature Caverns. Tigeraffe had back companions, which were eyes. So, if Tigeraffe was angry, he would shoot lasers. If he was happy, they would shoot out confetti. In Creature Caverns, there were lots of creatures, including Tigeraffe's worst nightmare, Evileraffe. Evileraffe was always trying to make Tigeraffe angry and sad. Evileraffe didn't realise that when Tigeraffe was angry, his minions would shoot lasers out of control. Tigeraffe told Evileraffe and they lived as friends forever.

Harris Anderson (10)
Parkhill Primary School, Leven

Frosty Howl

Frosty Howl was racing through space portals! New galaxies raced past him until he finally reached Ice Land. He confronted Sunny and the war began... Sunny is Howl's sworn enemy, they have been for ages!

"Come on Howl or are you too scared?"

"Are you challenging me? You are going to get it now Sunny."

Sunny and Howl fought day and night. Six days later, Howl's parents arrived. Suddenly Howl's ice breath went out of control and, disaster, Howl froze his parents! *Nooo!* He had frozen Sunny too, but in dismay he killed himself. Is this the end?

Kayden Foster (11)
Parkhill Primary School, Leven

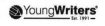

King Elyigousus' Cool Adventure

Suddenly, King Elyigousus emerged out of the cave and announced, "The cave is clear!"

They crawled through and came across a group of miners. They hurried away because humans are horrifying, and they escaped. After sneaking through a very tight jungle, they spotted a baby Elyigousus in trouble!

They came to it, but then, a net landed on them. They walked up on a boat trapped inside cages! Then, an explosion rattled the ship, bringing it down. Everyone escaped and swam to land. They were split by how they live in peace across many places across the world called Earth.

Shay Fisher (10)

Parkhill Primary School, Leven

Spotty Eagle

One day on Planet Sun, two little elves were getting picked on. The Spotty Eagle saw what was happening and ran over to help the elves. Spotty shouted to jump on his back, and the elves did. They ran to Wonderland, and the monsters ran after them. Then, in Wonderland, they bumped into Spotty's enemy, Stripy Eagle.

"What are you doing here?" said Stripy.

"We're here from the monsters," said the elves.

The monsters caught up to them and Spotty paused time, took the naughty goo out of them and unpaused time. The monsters turned into kind monsters.

Ashton Andrew Cunningham (10)

Parkhill Primary School, Leven

29

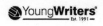

Untitled

I was watching TV when I saw the breaking news. "There is going to be a snowstorm on Friday, tomorrow, we've even received reports of this crazy creature. We do not know what or where he is. An unknown name. If you see this monster, call 911 as quickly as possible."

I did not believe it, but my annoying older brother said, "The news! The news! There's going to be a snowstorm tomorrow and a monster on the loose. Would you protect me?" shouting from his lungs. Then, that exact creature appeared at the window. The creature was standing there...

Harry Thomson (10)
Parkhill Primary School, Leven

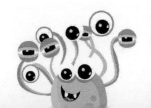

Robi The Robot

One day in a very hi-tech laboratory, scientists were trying to create artificial intelligence robots. During the creation, a mass explosion occurred and one of the robots had become evil and extremely angry and it was called Rageful Ruari. Two of the robots were friendly, and they were called Robi the Robot and Robotic Rory.
After Robi went back to Technomania his secret badge was vibrating. He looked through it and Rory was getting beaten up by Ruari. Robi went back to Earth and used his protect bubble around Rory and used his heal pulse to heal Rory up.

Jack O'Brien (10)
Parkhill Primary School, Leven

Fluffy And Rosey To The Rescue

One afternoon, Fluffy and Rosey went out for biscuits and tea. Suddenly, their friendship arrows started flashing. *That's not good*, they thought. They ran to see what was wrong and saw Brooke and Lucy had fallen out. Fluffy ran to Brooke while Rosey helped Lucy. Fluffy sat beside Brooke and gave her some biscuits, and Rosey had tea with Lucy.

The next morning, Rosey thought of a plan to make Lucy and Brooke friends again. They all went to the park and Fluffy and Rosey shot Brooke and Lucy with their friendship arrows. Hooray! Mission accomplished.

Zia Anderson (10)

Parkhill Primary School, Leven

Ice The Confidence Monster

Ice was helping kids with worries on their minds because of school. She wanted to help them be more confident, stop worrying and be happy and confident in school.

Then Ice saw a sad-looking little girl, worrying about a test she hadn't studied for. So, Ice gently held her hand, squeezed it tight and made her confident for her test. This squeeze helped and she successfully completed her mission.

She felt great and she had more children to help who were worried, angry, stressed, or just not confident. Ice was happy about all of her future missions to come.

Sara Grove (10)
Parkhill Primary School, Leven

Roller-Running

In Swirly Land it's the middle of the night. Rolly Polly is asleep, but then someone puts Rolly Polly into a sack. When Rolly Polly wakes up, he's ended up in Rocky Land. After a little while, Rolly Polly sees his enemy, Running Rocky. Rolly Polly starts taunting him. Then, Running Rocky starts charging at Rolly Polly. Rolly Polly just barely gets away. He's on the run - or, on the roll. When Rolly Polly stops, Running Rocky jumps from his back because Rocky is on his back riding Rolly Polly. Then Rolly Polly charges up and finally defeats Running Rocky.

Ruari Gibson (11)
Parkhill Primary School, Leven

Untitled

Zet was at his thirteenth birthday with his brothers. His dad had died and he had two sons. No one knew who the new king was because he had died. Zet found a map leading him to a treasure.

The first challenge was inside a monster's stomach. Zet would have to get the key off the monster's tongue. That was the most dangerous part of the monster.

The second challenge was that Zet had to dive into a volcano where the lava monster lived, ready to battle, and Zet had to defeat him to be king.

Delight Anyanwu (10)
Parkhill Primary School, Leven

Rocket Bot 3000's Big Adventure

It was a sunny day. Rocket Bots 3000 and 2000 are at home trying to find out which planet they come from because all they know is that they're best friends. When they try to check their settings it says, "*Error, error.*"

Suddenly, Rocket Bots 5000 and 4000 bust through the roof. Rocket Bot 3000 and 2000 fly away to the professor, away from Rocket Bots 4000 and 5000 and to find out where they are from.

Six days later, they make it and the professor says they are from Rotopia.

Kylar Boyce (10)
Parkhill Primary School, Leven

How The World Works

My name is Andrew and I was bullied a lot in school for being different. I am now fourteen years old and have learned to deal with unkind words that are said to me.

There were some boys in my class who would make fun of me for having two extra eyes. I would walk home, crying, until I did not have any more tears.

After a few months of being bullied, I finally worked up the courage to tell my teacher and, in less than a week, I started skipping, smiling and laughing all the way home.

Isla Lynch (10)
Parkhill Primary School, Leven

The Search For The Police

Suddenly, a bomb struck David and Dan's house. So they had to move to this strange High School called All-Star Academy. David was jealous that Dan was popular. So, he decided to call the alien police. But the next day, he regretted it. It was his enemy Scruff, they quickly ran as fast as they could. They decided to gang up on Scruff, but Scruff was in danger. This meant life or death. They quickly ran up to him and pushed him into a nearby bin.
"This is the end for you!"

Sophie Selbie (10)
Parkhill Primary School, Leven

Legend Of The North

Deep in the taigas of Scandinavia, a snowstorm raged overhead and sparks and embers flew as the Legend of the North, a mythical fire wolf, feasted on its prey. This was a photo opportunity too good to miss, I just hoped for dear life I wouldn't get eaten. Just as that thought came into my head I realised it had spotted me. It had a severe hate for humans and it let out a long, low growl as it sank its fangs into me. It then returned to its prey. I survived, but just.

Anthony Peter Celinski (10)
Parkhill Primary School, Leven

Bobby, The Healing Creature

Meet Bobby, he does not like dogs or cats, but he can heal people. Today, he had a mission. His mission was to help a girl who'd broken her arm and leg. Bobby was heading off to heal the girl, but on his way, there was a cat, but that didn't stop him. He just went around the cat. He finally made it to the girl. She was in a lot of pain, and it was hard to heal her, but he did heal her in the end and she felt so much better.

Jorgie Foster (11)
Parkhill Primary School, Leven

Sandy Brite

One day, I was walking to the park when I saw my friend, Sandy. We went to the park together. We sat down on a bench and had some ice cream, then we went to the arcade, where we saw my bullies. Sandy was angry because they tried to fight me. When Sandy saw that, we got into a fight. He joined in, and when my bullies hit him, he gulped one of them up and then another and then again, until none of them were left.

Rihanna Westwater (10)
Parkhill Primary School, Leven

Sapphire Whispers: A Girl's Quest For Nature's Magic

As I was strolling amongst an enshrouded, iridescent forest I approached a peculiar murmuring. What could it possibly be? Tiptoeing tentatively towards the chaotic commotion, I stumbled amidst a celestial feather, swaying within the blood-curdling breeze.

"Is anyone there?" my raspy voice echoed throughout the perilous atmosphere. The only sound I received was the rustle of the exotic magma-red leaves beneath my mud-splattered shoes.

"Squawk, it's nice to meet you!" A mesmerising bird infested with a cacophony of constellation feathers soared toward me.

"You're a talking bird?" I mumbled.

"What do you think? Come, this is where our adventure begins!"

Ava Chandarana (11)
Rothley CE Primary Academy, Rothley

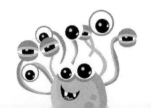

Skapizretr The Citizen Of Mazkin

In the playground of distant galaxies, Skapizretr was playing with friends, showing its extraordinary powers. With a mere thought, it conjured storms of stardust and shot lasers, but their happiness was interrupted when a nefarious abductor flew in with the goal of capturing Skapizretr's powers for his own use. Unfazed, Skapizretr unleashed its ability to spit anything it desired, sending torrents of molten lava towards the interloper. With a flick of his mind, Skapizretr ensnared his enemy in ethereal chains, making it powerless. Freed from captivity, Skapizretr and his friends celebrated at the universe's most esteemed restaurant, relishing in their marvellous victory.

Kaelan Patel (11)
Rothley CE Primary Academy, Rothley

The Twirling Monster

In a town called Woodsville, there was a deafening crash roaring over the homestead. Horror filled the faces of the villagers, their hearts palpitating, panting, and gasping. As the sound of monstrosity grew louder, the Woodsville community grew more alarmed. *Stomp, stomp, stomp!* Rushing to the village came a loathsome creature, coming to rescue this planet. As the dancing monster edged the town, she realised how tedious it was. She decided to turn the humans into poised ballet dancers. Things didn't go how the monster planned! They started destroying buildings and paintings. However, the not-so-twirling monster couldn't transform them back.

Nancy Greenhill (11)
Rothley CE Primary Academy, Rothley

The Hut

While the moonlit sky winked at the gleaming stream, lavender petals drifted through the warm, tranquil mist. Nonchalantly chewing, the brown-coated, furry creature embraced its surroundings: blossom hanging from the tall oak branches and tall, healthy trees towering to the inky roof above. Strolling, the animal stumbled upon a hut. A hut which had someone inside, someone with a tall, crooked hat and a long black robe. The mysterious silhouette was stirring a green, sloppy brew until she stopped, stopped and looked at the creature. "James, you're home!" yelled the witch. A warm, welcoming smile greeted the unicorn.

Imogen Hunter (11)

Rothley CE Primary Academy, Rothley

The Dragladon

I awake from my slumber, breathless; a stream of bitter sweat trickles down my pale face. My body aches intensely and I steady myself. A vast forest envelops me; towering trees overlook the rugged mountains. I absorb my surroundings. The ominous moon shines fiercely, revealing a perilous creature adjacent to me: a Dragladon. Its teeth are like deadly daggers. Its eyes like pools of fire. The Dragladon's colossal feet pound repetitively like my apprehensive heart. Its vicious eyes scan, oblivious to my whereabouts. One wrong move; I'd be dinner. Its ear-piercing screech echoes through the forest; my overwhelmed eyes blur.

Jude Rowley (11)
Rothley CE Primary Academy, Rothley

The Shadow Creature!

In the depths of a dark wood, a young girl stumbled upon a clearing. A mysterious sound pierced the air, it was so piercing, it was almost deafening. Cam, intrigued, crept closer. The noise screeched like nails on a chalkboard. Her heart pulsated.

What was that strange sound?

Where did it come from?

Was it a warning?

Palms sweating, Cam peered into a shaking bush. A squirrel shot out, making her fall. A ginormous shadow-like creature towered over her, growling. "Get out!"

Cam gasped, then ran. She saw the monster: big stumpy legs, long hairy arms and lines of spikes along its back.

Aria Tipping (11)
Rothley CE Primary Academy, Rothley

Waffle Vs Baby

In Strawberry Flower Land, Prince Waffle Bottom is jamming to his favourite tunes when he discovers his favourite creature.

Magical fairy Pikachu is in Pancakeville, five miles away.

Waffle sets off with Big, his unloyal flying fish, hoping to ride Pikachu. Near Pancakeville, Big Blue, an evil bubble, lands on Boss Baby, who is relaxing nearby. Weird noises follow, then *boom!* Boss Baby turns evil. Scared, Waffle tries to run away, but a fight ensues. Waffle wins by hitting Boss Baby with a book. Victorious, he flies home on Pikachu, while dancing to Beyoncé's 'All The Single Ladies'.

Bella Burgess (11)

Rothley CE Primary Academy, Rothley

The Sea Monster

Drifting across the sea, I come to a stop. As my sturdy piece of driftwood comes ashore on an unknown island, shivers crawl down my spine, leaving goosebumps to scatter around my body. I am lost. I am scared. I am uncertain what's going to happen.

In the distance, there is a humungous creature lurking throughout the mainland, in hopes of finding something tasty.

Splash! An enormous sea monster rises above human sight. "I'm here to help," announces the funny-looking beast.

Not knowing what to do, I step aboard the fluffy, pink spotty whale. I'm now back home where I belong.

Ava Brett-Pitt (11)
Rothley CE Primary Academy, Rothley

The Crawler

Everyone was worried sick. Jack's brother (Max) had ventured too far. He'd ventured into the Shadow Realm, where the Crawler lived. Everybody but Jack had given up; he was determined (luckily, he was a Marsling, or he wouldn't be able to feel his brother's emotions).

Later that night, he went looking. He went beyond the fence... it went dark. He wasn't far off. Jack travelled about one hundred metres and found Max. Disaster struck! Rocks fell! Every Marsling had powers; Max had telekinesis. He shifted the rocks and trekked home. Everyone was relieved and made Max promise to never leave again.

Isaac Allan (10)
Rothley CE Primary Academy, Rothley

The Fight

Once, there was a child exploring the forest when she stumbled upon a monster. She stood there, frozen, looking at the hairy but fluffy, clever but naughty, giant but yeti-like griffin.

She ran away in fear and told the settlement. The settlement prepared stone weapons to banish the yeti-like griffin.

"We set out at midnight," said the chief.

As they marched the monster followed behind the group, picking them off one by one until only the chief was left. *Thrash!* Lightning struck. As the chief turned around he saw the monster lying dead, on fire from the lightning strike. He cheered.

Archie Heald (11)
Rothley CE Primary Academy, Rothley

Bongo The Adventurer

Deep inside the Jam Pot Jungle stood a crazy purple creature called Bongo, who wore a cloak of shamrock-green scales. This creature had a secret craving - M&M's.

One sunny morning, he wisely chose to head to the M&M's shop in London, for he knew that this was chocolate heaven.

Ravenously, he darted across the Atlantic Ocean, up the River Thames and into the store where he found millions of mouth-watering M&M's.

He shoved them all into his wide mouth. Little did he know of the disaster that was about to occur - a life-ending allergic reaction.

Sad times, Bongo. Sad times.

Louis Burgess (11)
Rothley CE Primary Academy, Rothley

Bobalox Versus Coxyboxy

Deep in an enchanted forest, a brawl had begun. Bobalox versus Coxyboxy. Bobalox; twenty legs, fifty arms, ten eyes and the colour green versus Coxyboxy; who has a box for a head, is the colour brown and is very cocky.

The brawl had started because Bobalox had stolen Coxyboxy's football. Coxyboxy's anger erupted like a volcano and Coxyboxy powered at Bobalox. Bobalox shoved Coxyboxy to the ground. "That hurt!" muttered Coxyboxy.

The fight carried on until sunset. Bobalox had won by the barest of margins. Every onlooker called that battle, the battle of the century.

Ethan Wilkinson (11)
Rothley CE Primary Academy, Rothley

The Bizarre Woods

"Run!" I shout to my friend Steve, as I sprint as far away from the monster as I can.

Whilst we were adventuring through the forest, I'd spotted a creature out of the corner of my eye; it had four layers of razor-sharp teeth, it was as colossal as a giant, it was covered in hair from head to toe, and thorn-like spikes crawled up its back.

"I think we lost it," Steve whispers.

"But we're lost," I reply.

Suddenly, I hear footsteps. *Thump!* Then I turn around. It's the monster.

Beep! Beep! Beep! It was only a dream - phew.

Dylan Tailor (11)

Rothley CE Primary Academy, Rothley

Bouncer And The Flyer

The Blue Bouncer is an outcast living in the wrong world. He was born in a dream, with iridescent skylines dancing on the sunset's symphonies. The people were as bright as the sun.

But that was then, and now he's on Earth, with polluted breeze and dilapidated buildings. His dream is to return to Zortron.

He's been planning for years to breathe the same air as the people back home. Today, he will.

He prepares his rocket, says one last goodbye to this unloving world, and... *Click*. The oval-shaped ship slices through space: he arrives. His mood bounces around the air...

Lucas Dowdall-Branston (11)
Rothley CE Primary Academy, Rothley

The Unexpected Night

One unilluminated night, Esme knew time wasn't going too brisk. She had an idea to bake. Whilst in the kitchen she stumbled across a gleam that caught her attention. It led to her dazzling garden. She was too stunned to speak as light swallowed. Esme screamed with terror. "What is that?" she cried. A six-legged creature with a purple coat, three eyes and unbelievably good dance moves greeted her with an awfully embarrassing accent. "G'day kiddo, come with me for an unforgettable night." And off she went to another universe and had an unexplainable night.

Layla Sutton (11)
Rothley CE Primary Academy, Rothley

The Umibozu

The Umibozu lurks in the cold melancholy ocean depths only rising to sink Japanese ships.
One day, a ship came sailing over uncharted seas. The Umibozu's chance was now. Suddenly, the blue void started shaking and lightning struck from above. The Umibozu rose from the depths and confronted the sailors. Their boat sank and was never seen again. This all happened to sailors for decades until, one day, the Umibozu rose out of the water. The tempestuous seas grazed against the side of the boat. The steward presented it with a bottomless bucket. It went away and never came back... until today.

Sebastian Springthorpe (11)
Rothley CE Primary Academy, Rothley

Untitled

As the nonchalant wind tickled the branches of the luminous trees, the crystal-clear water relaxed lackadaisically. The sun's rays touched the water, leaving an iridescent shimmer. Pink petals drifted in the morning peace. All was quiet.

All was quiet apart from the snap of a twig under someone's foot. The twig snap belonged to a creature; it had a body like a lizard with pink scales, a dominating tail and crimson, puckered lips. It was definitely a zogg.

The expression on the woman's face changed as she looked him up and down. She had never seen something like this before.

Esmé Endacott (10)
Rothley CE Primary Academy, Rothley

Untitled

This is my mythical creature called Fin John Slapmore. The searing, oppressive, golden sphere had arms the size of the Eiffel Tower that could punch a single person into outer space. It had seven pupils, which could analyse any perilous accidents or possibly war. Descending below the waist, there were four wiggly, bubbly, lime-green legs that could strangle and decapitate anything in its path. Finally, the blinding light of the beaming tyrant could knock out anyone who looked at it. The acrimonious scold of the shiny trophy could give someone nightmares for the rest of their lives - deadly.

Luca Smart
Rothley CE Primary Academy, Rothley

The Creature In The Woods

As Maya ran through the dense thicket, her tawny waistcoat caught onto an offshoot and the thorns of fallen branches scraped across her back. Brandishing her dagger, she cut herself free. Maya carried on but stopped. She knew it had found her. The hairs on her neck stood up; faint sounds of footsteps treading across the sodden ground became louder. Someone or something was following her. A wet hand brushed her shoulder. She turned. The creature had bones bulging out of its jet-black skin. Its face half melted. She had to run; her legs were frozen. Everything soon went black.

Sienna Sandhu (11)
Rothley CE Primary Academy, Rothley

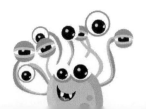

The Girasus

My crazy creature is a Girasus. The head and neck of a giraffe and the body of a pegasus. Now, this story is short but tragic.

This story all started in the Girasus' cave where his three most prized possessions, his eggs, or as humans like to call them, death traps, got murdered...

So, as the villagers were terrified of these death traps, they killed all three eggs. The Girasus was fuming, so he paid his rent, and then Girasus (Steve) travelled long and far with his mighty wings to the village and just bought three more to scramble or boil or, perhaps, poach.

Millie Morris (11)

Rothley CE Primary Academy, Rothley

The Giants' Wrath

As the giants' massive feet crashed down on the Earth, buildings fell, crumbling to the ground. One of the giants' feet stood on the remaining rubble. People ran for safety, trying to avoid the giants' wrath and praying to avoid death.

The giant didn't care what became of the people below him; all that he cared about was destruction, death, and making the world his own. The humans ran for cover as they let the tanks do the job. 3, 2, 1, fire! *Boom!* The giants retreated to the horrible planet they call home. Humanity is safe... for now.

Kian Norton (10)
Rothley CE Primary Academy, Rothley

You Never Know What's In The Dark

If the room is as dark as a raven's wing then you know that anything could be lurking within. The creaking of the floorboards, the rusting of the screws and the pungent aroma in the air indicate there is more to the story than an abandoned toy factory.

Sitting inconspicuously on a grimy shelf is a teddy bear. As the sun sets, a shadow is cast upon the toy, revealing a frightful fact – it is alive.

Unexpectedly, the bear leaps from his perch, clapping his paws and waking all the toys in the deserted factory.

There is no escaping. I am trapped.

Phoebe McKinlay (10)
Rothley CE Primary Academy, Rothley

The Goblin Who Was Hungry

One night, I was on my phone eating cookies and drinking some milk in my kitchen when suddenly a cold breeze trickled up my spine. I was positive that no windows or doors were open. I got up out of my seat, and then, *bang!* A six-legged goblin leapt out through my window.

"G'day, mate." The goblin spoke with an Australian accent. "Don't mind me just trying to find some food."

My jaw plummeted to the ground. The goblin had a long red cape and four antennas. He grabbed my cookies and leapt out the window, and that was that!

Lucia Alonzi (11)
Rothley CE Primary Academy, Rothley

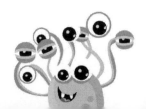

The Peculiar Evening At The Underwater Inn

In the darkest depths of the sea, down a deep and dark trench, through a doorway made of coral, was the Underwater Inn. As soon as I walked in, my eardrums were drowned in sound. The chitter-chattering, the smooth ba-dum of the bass and the clinking of drinks. Suddenly, the stage erupted into light! It was Irving Murphy, the famous squid-faced singer from The Big Pacific newspaper. "Good evening, fellow sailors and sea creatures," he purred. "Tonight I will perform Haul on the Bowline, with the high note. *Tink!* The glass enclosure shattered.

Ruth Brown (10)
Rothley CE Primary Academy, Rothley

The Girl In Red

As the sun cracked open its appeal, the Girl in Red entered the noble giant's domain, forlorn, away from any connection to the real world. She was here for the fight of the century against the Girl of Red.

Dragging behind her death-eating dagger, a malevolent smirk filled her face, squelching mud rang in the witch's ears. Peering through a haggard, weary bush, there she saw the Girl of Red.

Suddenly, she had a cruel idea. Her mind hurled a rock through the air, leaving a pool of blood behind. She stood in front of the city, victorious.

Sofia Hanmer (11)
Rothley CE Primary Academy, Rothley

Monster School Trip

Jaffrez and his monster friends were on a school trip. They were visiting Alpzzaola. A place where enchanted colours and indigo sky awaken your soul and mythical creatures jive through the ominous abyss. Jaffruz and his friends, Spiky and Spooky decided to go and explore a swamp they found. As they watched the swamp bubble and ooze, a chill marched down their spine. They all knew something was off. Suddenly, a pack of unrecognisable monsters started to crawl out of the swamp and began to growl, but it was just then Mum called for Freddie to wake up.

Freddie Lines (11)
Rothley CE Primary Academy, Rothley

The Takeover

The demonic souls are trapped in the deep hole of darkness, where all light fades to dust. Creepy creatures guard the god Zeus, mythical legends who created all history to be crushed, by the ruler of Hell... Lucifer. Jimmy is just a normal boy who has a regular life, but one day, he was flying his drone up a mountain when something off it was all destroyed: cracks in the ground, but a sword. Jimmy was intrigued by his discovery but saw a demon. He did not hesitate to pick up the sword and swung, dead.

"I need to battle Lucifer."

George Harrison (10)

Rothley CE Primary Academy, Rothley

The Frog, The Cane And The Pond

A frog, an innocent animal, the most boring of its kind. Or is it?

Today I saw the most peculiar thing. An astounding amphibian wearing the classiest clothes imaginable; a top hat, a monocle and a fine cane. I tracked him down to see where he was going and he came to a stop right outside the mucky and grimy fish pond.

"My home! It's ruined!" he exclaimed.

Then, I don't know what I saw, but before my eyes, with one tap of his cane, he was gone. And as for the fish pond, well, that turned into a beautiful lake.

Toby Suart (10)
Rothley CE Primary Academy, Rothley

Crazy Creatures

Yo, whatsup, I'm Leo, the weirdest thing happened to me. So I was hiking in a woodland area, I heard strange noises. I tried to ignore them, but it sounded like it was coming closer and closer. It stopped. A shadow began to form in front of me. I began to run, the blood-sucking alien thing that looked like it was from Harry Potter, ran at me. After picking me up, he put me in a well with my journal.

Little did I know this: the well is infested with human-eating ants, and they all have over 1 billion eyes and scorpion tails.

Leo Marlow (11)

Rothley CE Primary Academy, Rothley

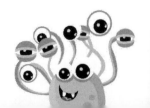

Gliserdon Paradise

The enraptured creature with an idyllic personality: the glisten in her eyes, staring at your thighs. Shimmers on her coat, daisies in her ears, as the Gliserdon gallops, it reads your fears. She lives in a place, a place like no other: lilypads dancing and dandelions prancing. A favourite for all, luscious wet grass, the elegant gleam that no one's ever seen. When the gleeful Gliserdon is full of content, rainbows blasting out, but none for rent.
"There are only a few to see... Do you think you can spot me?"

Aura Williams (10)
Rothley CE Primary Academy, Rothley

The Girl Of Red

The forest was thick with trees, yet seemed forlorn and dilapidated. She was there for one reason and one reason only: to kill the girl in red.

As the ground squelched under her feet, she heard a susurrus from the trees. It was her – the girl in red, a witch.

She was not afraid of the girl in red, for she was also a witch, and the girl in red's power of telekinesis was nothing compared to her fireballs, but something hit her in the back of the head. A rock.

A pool of blood appeared. She was dead.

Elizabeth Brunt (11)
Rothley CE Primary Academy, Rothley

Crazy Creature

One ominous, gloomy night a young girl ventured into the forest. Cautiously strolling through the emerald nature she caught a sharp glance of a cerulean spike poking out of the tree which lay in front of her. She walked closer, only to find five beady eyes transfixed on her, a set of bloodthirsty teeth ready to strike and a huge wart at the end of its nose. The young girl was absolutely speechless and her heart was beating at such a pace it felt like it might pop out of her chest. She had no other option but to run!

Mila Higginson (10)
Rothley CE Primary Academy, Rothley

73

The Cat Who Brought In A Frog

At one o'clock in the morning, I suddenly woke up to a deep meow. I closed my eyes and went back to sleep, thinking it was nothing. Then I heard an ear-piercing scream! I quickly jumped out of bed and ran down the stairs and looked around my house. I came across my naughty grey cat (Bo) who was peering under the sofa. I looked under the sofa with my bright torch and saw small eyes staring back at me! I stepped away in shock. The eyes emerged from under the sofa, then I realised... it was a slimy frog!

Freya Sharpe (11)
Rothley CE Primary Academy, Rothley

The Catastrophski

It was a cold winter night; the snow was relentless, like a blanket over the Alaskan Highlands. Max awoke from his slumber in his cosy log cabin, startled by the noise that boomed outside. Max jumped out of bed in his warm cotton pyjamas, sprinted across his cabin, and flung open the door. Max peered down the snow-covered mountain at the scene that unfolded before him. His pet cat, which was fluffy with orange fur, was skiing down the side of the mountain with a menagerie of animals cheering him on.

Seb Seed
Rothley CE Primary Academy, Rothley

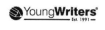
The Darkness Within

In the dark, all alone, I stay in a sombre abandoned mineshaft with my colossal black body and my long, lanky, black, hairy legs. As I sit on my immense pile of gold and sapphire, guarding it like my life depends on it, I hear heavy footsteps. I dig my tense legs into the ground. My back sticks up, my eyes glow red and my hairs stand up. As the shadow gets closer I realise it is pest control! Run! I swing and shoot webs all over the place, running as fast as I can but suddenly I'm caught. Oops!

Jacob Sullinskozicki (11)
Rothley CE Primary Academy, Rothley

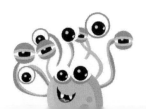

The Gnome With No Home

Garry, the gnome, had a problem; he didn't have a sense of smell, as he was born without a nose. He didn't realise that he was pongy and, as a result, he was told to leave the Gnome Kingdom. Off he went on a quest to find a new home. On his travels, he came across a weird creature. It had a green body, three antennas, seven eyes and blue hair. He looked scary at first but Gary didn't judge creatures by their appearance. The creature was grateful and offered Garry a home.

Macie Bentley (11)
Rothley CE Primary Academy, Rothley

The Zooming Pup

As usual, at 10am, she went for her daily stroll, but today was different. She came across a bottle and she drank it. Skates appeared on each of her four paws. She was zooming, sniffing and loving life. Charging down the hill, something was going to go wrong! As she approached the dead end, she took off. She closed her eyes, hoping for the best. There was no crash, no bang. She opened her eyes, and there she was in her cosy doggy basket. Had it all been a dream?

Lottie Pritchard (11)
Rothley CE Primary Academy, Rothley

The Very Strange Cat

One day, there was a cat who was strange, a cat who was different. This cat wouldn't go catching things. He would lick glue all day, and in the winter he would eat snow. He liked being on a leash like a dog.

This cat needed to go to the vet because he had come home with a rubber in his mouth. He went to the vet and then he was normal again. He needed a shot in the leg, and it was amazing. He would go on to catch rats and he would not go on walks again.

Anaya Joshi (11)

Rothley CE Primary Academy, Rothley

The Wormhole Monster

I was walking in a melancholy woodland when, all of a sudden, I saw a three-horned monster who was nine feet tall and had a long peach and white tail.

It was trying to suck me into a mysterious wormhole. The wormhole had an almighty pull.

I have no idea what went on that day and I don't want to learn more about that monster.

Shayan Mashru (11)
Rothley CE Primary Academy, Rothley

Jon The Terror

Jon is a fierce creature with sharp claws and sharp teeth. If Jon sees a rat, he will chase after the rat. Jon strikes no fear in other creatures. Jon is also a greedy creature and will eat anything. Jon likes to go into the garden every day, and last but not least, Jon is a good cat.

Arthur Warner (11)
Rothley CE Primary Academy, Rothley

The Dancing Plant

Once, I was strolling in the woods and then something came out of the bush and started dancing. Then a pair of hands popped out of the plant and started wiggling, then the music started to play.
Honestly, I thought that night I was hallucinating.

Filip Jasinski (11)
Rothley CE Primary Academy, Rothley

The Greatest Hero Of All Time

Boktowolf, a violet, short-haired, three-eyed creature, was born on Planet Earth. At first glance, Bokto thought Earth was a pleasant place. Bokto's fluffy, spotty mum signed Bokto up for human school. Bokto was thrilled.
"Thanks, Mum."
It was Bokto's first day, and as he walked into school, whispers and rumours were being told.
"Will you be my friend?" wailed Bokto to the bully.
The bully answered, "No, hideous monster."
As Bokto cried in the corner, he saw a little kid fall from a ten-storey building. He managed to catch her, and everybody started to cheer.
"He's so loving. We are sorry!"

Lola Clark (10)
Springfield Community Primary School, Burnley

The Day Angle Had A Problem

In Odd World, lived a monster named Angle and Angle loved his world. Until one day Angle came across a problem.

"Mummy!" said Angle.

"Yes, my dear?" Mum replied.

"I want to go to Earth in my spaceship," said Angle.

"Okay love," Mum said.

Angle went outside to get his spaceship. But when Angle put the key in to start it, it didn't work. Angle started to cry. But his sister, Arlo, came to the rescue.

"You okay brother?" said Arlo.

"No, my spaceship won't work," said Angle.

"It's okay, just use mine," said Arlo.

"Yay!" shouted Angle.

Abigail Warren (9)
Springfield Community Primary School, Burnley

Mr Cyclicon And The Loud Mouthed Monsters

Once, a thousand years ago, intergalactic space aliens were peacefully living in the inter-world. But, one day, their enemies, the monsters, were making too much noise. Then something appeared in the atmosphere. It was spherical, futuristic and had a series of mechanical levers and complex switches. It was a mothership!
It landed on our planet, and then a mysterious being emerged. Its name was Mr Cyclicon. He said he would stop the noise coming from the monsters. So he went into his ship, which swiftly advanced towards the monsters. He stopped the loud noise coming from the monsters. Job well done!

Aarav Kataria (10)
Springfield Community Primary School, Burnley

Mr Four Eyes And The Fire-Breathing Dragon

On Planet Five Eyes, Mr Four Eyes, who was being bullied about his appearance, went to another planet, not realising he was going to make the biggest mistake of his life. Everyone on the planet was afraid to travel around space, but Mr Four Eyes didn't see why. Arriving at the planet, he saw a huge, fire-breathing dragon! Bursting with nerves, he managed to hide behind a massive rock, giving him enough time to shape-shift into a dragon and get away. Thankfully, he survived and got home, where he was congratulated, was never bullied again and was treated like a hero.

Adam Ahmed (10)
Springfield Community Primary School, Burnley

Tommy Gets A Friend

Once, in Mighty Monster Village, lived a fluffy monster called Tommy. Tommy had no friends and was very lonely. One day, he took out his magic globe and found a lonely little girl called Darcey. She had no friends either, so Tommy decided to make a rocket to Earth. He gave his mummy, daddy and sisters a big hug and *blast off!* He travelled to Earth.

He knocked on Darcey's door. As she opened the door, she picked him up in shock and gave him the biggest hug.

Now they're both so happy that they have finally got a best friend. *Yay!*

Hallie Noone (9)

Springfield Community Primary School, Burnley

Enemies To Best Friends

Blugy is a human/bug who lives in Buggy Town and has an enemy called Ralph. Blugy has a power and gets bullied for it. That's why they're enemies. The power is that he can shoot rainbows out of his hands. He hates his power and he just wants a friend.

One day, Ralph was playing and a boy from another class was really mean to him.

Suddenly, something unexpected happened. Blugy went to help him. At first, he was confused because they're enemies, but in the end, he let him help and they're inseparable now and they love each other.

Maisy Davison (9)

Springfield Community Primary School, Burnley

The Befriending Of A Dragon

On Planet Pluto lived Mr Davil, who had a long arm and a hand at the bottom. He was flying to the ice cream shop to order ice cream. Afterwards, he was looking at Earth, in the blink of an eye he was in his dad's spaceship. His eyes set on Earth and eventually he arrived at the desert. But he was low on fuel, then Mr Saage, the dragon, Mr Devil's enemy, showed up. It breathed fire on Mr Devil's spaceship. It was too hot to fly, so he flew away the next day. He brought meat, Mr Saage's favourite, and they became best friends.

Jonathan Varela (10)
Springfield Community Primary School, Burnley

Plutovilla And The Meteorite

Once in Plutovilla, lived a monster called Mr Joles, who had green eyes with a colossal body. One day a meteorite destroyed Plutovilla. Everyone was shocked, no one knew how to fix it. However, Mr Joles had an idea. This idea was going to Earth in a rocket ship he had built.

He left the next day and landed in an immense building. Inside he met an engineer and told him what happened. He felt bad and decided to go with Mr Joles. Over the next week, the engineer and Mr Joles fixed Plutovilla so that it was normal again. Hooray!

Zuha Daud (10)
Springfield Community Primary School, Burnley

Zaza's Hair

Zaza, who was a bright yellow hairy monster, lived on a planet called Monster World. Zaza was quite happy with her life, however people would bully her because of how spiky and tangled her hair was. That made her feel very upset.

One day, Zaza went up to her mum in disappointment, telling her that she didn't like her hair and that she wanted to cut it all off.

"Zaza, your hair is what makes you special but we can cut it if you want," said Mum.

So she got a haircut and was never bullied ever again.

Zaineb Muhammad (10)
Springfield Community Primary School, Burnley

Sorry

Far away lived a yeti called Fafa. She was no ordinary yeti. She had the power to fix things easily.

Excitedly, Fafa landed on Earth in a girl's garden. Fafa was bored. To her right, she saw a very delightful ball. Happily, she started bouncing the ball. She couldn't stop it. Then she accidentally popped it. It made the girl cry non-stop. She quickly fixed it with her sticky slime and said sorry. The girl jumped on Fafa, hugged her, and said, "It's okay!"

Always say sorry; it gets the job done!

Saffa Sadiq (10)
Springfield Community Primary School, Burnley

Blossom And Her Crazy Cousins

One day, Blossom, who is very charitable, landed at a school with her crazy cousins. When it was lunchtime, Blossom helped the children, but it was really hard because they were dancing.

The kids spat the food and nearly choked. Then it was art time, so Blossom helped the teacher hand out water. However, Blossom's cousins spilt water on the art and the kids cried. Luckily, Blossom put towels on the art and saved it. The kids happily hugged Blossom. Blossom and the kids said bye.

Teodora Georgieva (10)
Springfield Community Primary School, Burnley

93

Don't Mess With Lightning

Long ago, in the wonderful land of Vontrana, which was very rich, there was a giant, glorious, strong shape-shifting dragon, who lived on Mount Moon. He lived in peace with the green, slimy aliens. This was until they charged at his enormous silver mountain, trying to shoot it down. Bravely, the people on Earth came to help. After a long time fighting Lightning, who was the dragon, the people won. Then they became best friends.

Willson Crowther (10)
Springfield Community Primary School, Burnley

Tangos Meets A New Friend

Tangos Marangos who lived on Mars for thirty-one quadrillion years, had a plan to go to Earth because everybody had three eyes but Marangos had two eyes. He arrived on Earth with excitement to meet a new friend called Max. He devastatingly spotted an enemy from Mars destroying the city. Quickly, Tangos Marangos jumped to the rescue! The city was saved and everybody lived happily since. Yay!

Nikola Kotsev (9)
Springfield Community Primary School, Burnley

The Moving Planet

Once, in Marsvilla lived a monster who had purple eyes, horns and beautiful wings. He played games and always had fun. But one day, the ground started to shake, but Mr Griffin had an amazing idea. He found a friend from Pluto that had telekinesis. He tried and tried to move the colossal planet, and he finally did. Then, after that the two monsters became friends ever since that moment.

Connie Ellerton (10)
Springfield Community Primary School, Burnley

Alex

On the planet Zuse lived a rare little creature called Alex.

One day, he accidentally snapped one of his horns, but when he went home his parents didn't recognise him, so they kicked him out. Alex was very sad, but determined to find a new home. Then he found Earth. He was over the moon.

Kelly Peek (10)
Springfield Community Primary School, Burnley

YoungWriters®
— Est. 1991 —

Fortune's Worth

Once upon a time, Fortune lived in a modest home, burdened by endless chores, whilst her brother enjoyed school and fashionable clothes. Despite her ragged attire, she had determination. Saving every golden tear as a testament to her dreams. Whispering wishes to the silent walls, she vowed to always respect and love everyone. Each day, she scrubbed floors, resolve unyielding.

One day, her golden tears caught the sunlight, casting a radiant glow. At that moment, Fortune realised her tears were not a curse but a promise of triumph with renewed hope. She continued her journey towards greatness with joy and happiness.

Talitha Mtawali (11)
St George's (VC) CE Primary School & Nursery, Kidderminster

Untitled

There was an announcement. It said that rivers were drying up and they didn't know why.

After that, Gloobigus went to a river. Suddenly, he saw the problem. There was a person. He looked happy.

The person said, "Haha, one more to go!"

Gloobigus knew what happened and he said, "Why are you taking water from us? Because we're running out!"

"Ha! This bucket has all the water then."

Gloobigus said, "Put it down!"

The person said, "Fine." And ran away.

Then he saw a medal. It was a trick. He won a medal from the Planets Trust.

Ezza Anwar Anwar (9)

St George's (VC) CE Primary School & Nursery, Kidderminster

Jiggly Puff Had No Friends

Once upon a time, there were two little monsters named Jiggly Puff and Daisie. They were enemies but, one day, Jiggly Puff said, "Daisie, can you be my friend?"
Daisie said, "No. Why would I want to be your friend?"
Jiggly Puff said, "Because I want a friend."
"Well, I don't care if you have friends or not. You are still not my friend. You're very, very, very mean," Daisie said to Jiggly Puff angrily.
Then one day Daisie said, "Do you want to be my friend now?"
Jiggly Puff said, "Yes."

Tiarna Walker (8)
St George's (VC) CE Primary School & Nursery, Kidderminster

The Hunt Of The Night

The night hunters were on the move. They were merciless, they were monsters. One stood out, a living nightmare. His blade was free from purity. He was searching, searching for someone who could reassure his goal was completed. Each bloody slaughter held a new skill. It made him even stronger. He had found his prey and he drew his blade. Conscious of the situation, his prey tried to escape its inevitable fate. It was impossible. Blood. It was everywhere. He completed his mission. He earned a new skill. His expression was that of a killer. He was the Dark Knight.

Syeda Sadiqa Ahmed (10)
St George's (VC) CE Primary School & Nursery, Kidderminster

Lulu And Her New Friends

Lulu is just another regular monster in Sparkly Flower Land, where everyone loves flowers. Lulu has two enemies, Jonah and Fifi. Jonah calls Lulu names, and Fifi bullies her. Lulu lives with her mum and dad. She has a twin brother, Milo. One day at school, she forgets her lunch and goes back. Then suddenly, there is an emergency, and someone from a land that hates flowers starts destroying them. Lulu and her enemies have to work together. Hours pass by, and they stop the intruder, and then they all become good friends and make up.

Aleema Begum (10)
St George's (VC) CE Primary School & Nursery, Kidderminster

About Sigi

My crazy monster has long red devil horns and an angel hoop around her head. Sigi has three eyes and big white wings. Her face has three mouths, one with vampire teeth, one with goofy, slimy teeth and one with a long tongue. She also has big claws.

She is really nice and very positive. If you be nice to her she can give you anything you want. She can also jump really high and flies really fast and runs fast. She also is a great flyer. She can also teleport and shape-shift. Sigi lives on an enormous, green mountain.

Sameera Khatun (8)
St George's (VC) CE Primary School & Nursery, Kidderminster

The Mysterious Yeti Dragon

One day, there lived a yeti and a dragon who were best friends and one day, they went to visit a mysterious cave that had a note that said 'dangerous'. Of course, they went in and he saw a machine. They went inside the machine as a combined yeti dragon. It was red and blue with black spots all over its body with five eyes, one big mouth, three feet with three big hairy toes and no hands. Its special yeti dragon powers were its ice fire breath and ear glow, which glowed really red, pointing bright and high.

Chase Alexander Reeves (7)
St George's (VC) CE Primary School & Nursery, Kidderminster

Exploring Bewdley

One morning, Sassy Bear and Daisy wanted to explore Bewdley. They got their backpacks and packed what they needed. When they set out, Daisy was getting hungry because she did not eat breakfast.

"Let's go to the shops and buy food," said Sassy Bear calmly.

"I am feeling hungry, so let's go," said Daisy.

When they reached home they saw their door open. They checked the house, but nothing was missing, so they instead went to bed softly and calmly, falling into a deep sleep.

Zakiya Ahmed (8)
St George's (VC) CE Primary School & Nursery, Kidderminster

Crazy Creature

I have got a crazy creature as a pet, it is a girl called Izzy. She is fluffy and pink. She is clever, friendly and pretty. She has five eyes and a big mouth. I love playing with her, and we play mermaids in the bath. She sleeps in her own bed by me. Izzy is short and sometimes naughty. She tries to fly, but she can't. We do everything together.

She came to school with me, and she played with my friends. No one was scared of her. She had fun with us, and we will be best friends forever.

Katlyn Hussey (10)
St George's (VC) CE Primary School & Nursery, Kidderminster

Crazy Creatures

My crazy creature is a scary one and is a boy called Freddie Fazbear. He is very short and scruffy and people are frightened of him, but he is my friend. He is brown and he has holes in him. He comes from a scary movie that I like. He has a big mouth and eyes. We play together and he sleeps in my room. He wears a hat and a bow, he is sometimes evil and good. He is a bear and he has sharp claws to scratch with when he gets mad. He has a microphone. He has got Freddie.

Junior (Steven) Hussey (9)
St George's (VC) CE Primary School & Nursery, Kidderminster

Aleen Kidnaps The Girls!

One day, me, Bobbi, Joey and Aisha all go to the cinema. Then when we are almost there we stumble across a big green alien and we all try to run but the alien grabs us with his lasers. Then he pulls us up with his flying car and in the blink of an eye we end up in a great big dark room, an escape room. We have to put our strengths together to work out how we're going to get out and then we finally do it and the alien gives us some gold.

Maicey Tilling (11)
St George's (VC) CE Primary School & Nursery, Kidderminster

Flying Head

It's a mythical creature. The name of my creature is Flying Head. It lives in a forest. It has hair with sharp teeth and long wings. This creature is hungry for human flesh. The interesting thing about my creature is that it's difficult to kill it. It makes me laugh when I think about it.

Anureet Kaur (8)
St George's (VC) CE Primary School & Nursery, Kidderminster

109

Nep's Dance Victory

On a faraway planet, there was a bright alien named Nep. Nep was really good at dancing and doing flips.

One day, Nep met a mean man named Bob, who was jealous. Nep beat Bob in a dance contest and everyone was happy again.

Timur Turan (8)

St George's (VC) CE Primary School & Nursery, Kidderminster

The True Wonder Ending!

"This is it Wonder," said Coomba. "This is the final level, so let's do this!" The final level was called This Is The Final Level. As Wonder entered the level they were in a room with nine mystery boxes and each one would teleport him to a calling. They encouraged themselves and defeated each boss. Nine bosses later, "We're done Coomba, we've done it!"
"No we haven't Wonder!"
"Mwahahahahahaha!"
"Let's defeat Towser!" shouted Wonder (even though he had the invincibility leaf power up, three hits and Towser was gone!) Top of the goal pole...

Alex Cripps (10)
Stow On The Wold Primary School, Stow On The Wold

111

The Competition

In Cloudy Haven, Artic Cloud School had their usual morning assembly. The headteacher, who was Wobblop's auntie, said, "There's a competition for the most sporty monster."

Wobblops and Klawvia immediately raised their hands. They glared at each other, and the competition began. Points added up and the scores were tied!

There were no challenges left. They had to split a prize. The teachers had a talk, and they decided that Wobblops deserved the award because Klawvia was selfish. After a while, Klawvia came over to Wobblops and said sorry for being selfish, but Wobblops ended up forgiving him.

Mollie Tustin (10)

Stow On The Wold Primary School, Stow On The Wold

Love Across Planets

In the dimness of Mars and the swirling dust storms lived Tilly, a gentle monster with luminous eyes. Loneliness surrounded her until she met Maxie, an adventurous human astronaut. His curiosity led him to Tilly's cave, where their worlds collided. Tilly's heartbeat quickened at his presence. When they looked at each other, Tilly's telepathy sparked. Despite their differences, love blossomed between the unlikely pair. But as the stars watched their forbidden bond, they faced cruel reality. Mars and Earth were their dividers. Yet, in each other's arms, they found hope, defying the cosmic odds.

Bethany Antiojo (10)
Stow On The Wold Primary School, Stow On The Wold

Elements Are Enemies

Inferno Ball lives in the land of exciting elements. Inferno Ball and his friend are enjoying playing games, when his nemesis elements, Ice and Water, come and interrupt. They try chasing Inferno Ball to destroy him, as they are scared he will evaporate them. They manage to catch his wing, which makes it disappear from their cold touches. He runs away, up to the volcano, and sees baby Ice. She looks like she might jump in. Inferno Ball saves Baby Ice. Water and Ice see and try thanking Inferno Ball by helping him grow back his wing. Now elements aren't enemies.

Harrison Jones (10)
Stow On The Wold Primary School, Stow On The Wold

My New Life

I'm Zoe, and I'm a type of monster called a shape-shifter. I had to move from my house in Italy to a place called Monsterany (the humans were getting suspicious of me).

The first day at my new school, my monster life was very scary. I took some deep breaths, worrying if I'd make new friends and settle in. Ahead, I saw what looked like another shape-shifter. It was! She was called Lucy. Lucy and I were always together, especially against the school's mean girls, Rose and Jenny. Despite them, I finally felt at home in my shape-shifting body.

Ella Goode (11)
Stow On The Wold Primary School, Stow On The Wold

Bulldoze Bullying

Ruby Dino was a cheeky character, and she had a stripy tummy, poofy hands and spikes along her back and an enemy! Chalky Charlie!
One ordinary Tuesday, Ruby Dino was bullied by Chalky Charlie. Ruby got really sad and started crying. Little did she know she'd disappeared. A little gremlin with a snake-like tongue and a big mouth came over and made her feel better! Ruby did the right thing; she told the headmistress what had happened. On Wednesday, Ruby Dino went to find Charlie, but he was suspended. Ruby has remembered bullying is unacceptable.

Lily O'Kane (11)
Stow On The Wold Primary School, Stow On The Wold

Untitled

Earth is having a major breakout. They're introducing a new type of species. It has a wobbly-shaped head and eleven bloodshot eyes. Everyone is scared of it because it has fire horns. No one knows why everyone is scared about it. They've heard that it is gentle and kind, and when it gets scared, its eyeballs fall out and come around the creature's head. The species' name is Wobbly Eyeballs Threat. That's why everyone is scared of them because of their name. This species cost £10,000 because of their wobbly head and wibbly eyes.

Gracie Adams (10)
Stow On The Wold Primary School, Stow On The Wold

Nightmares Get Stopped

Zoomblers are funny creatures. They like to lurk in the dark, but here's a Zoombler that protects the Earth. Jeff is from Planet Zoom and he is the best at missions. Jeff's mission was to save Earth. Jeff flew down as fast as a cheetah. He saw nightmare creatures, the flying Gloops. He sucked them up with a swoosh. Fearless Gloop smashed him to the ground and Fearless Gloop was his enemy. Jeff's horns grew larger than an elephant and then Jeff did the most powerful suck he has ever done, the other Gloops retreated so his job was done!

Eric Rothera (10)
Stow On The Wold Primary School, Stow On The Wold

Doughnut Days

Demon Doughnut was minding his own business, when suddenly, he looked down and noticed he couldn't see his leg. He blinked to see if he was imagining it. He was teleported to a different bakery. He looked around and realised it was Bagel Boy's home. His enemy! He saw a shadow. He flew towards it. Suddenly, Bagel Boy jumped out and broke his pitchfork. Enraged, Demon Doughnut jumped onto Bagel Boy and threw sprinkles at him. A giant claw picked up Demon Doughnut. When he thought he was dead, a human picked Bagel Boy up and ate him. Yummy!

Kush Kennedy (10)
Stow On The Wold Primary School, Stow On The Wold

119

Chickendog's Dream Mission

On Earth, Chickendog always wanted to go to weird and wonderful outer space. As fearless as ever, Chickendog went on a rocket. Chickendog was sent to fulfil his dream. As he arrived, he spotted Bagel Boy, his worst enemy. Chickendog ran as fast as his super-sharp talons could take him. When he arrived on Mars, the aliens came over to greet him. After they greeted Chickendog, he went round to explore. After a while, he made a friend, Bob, an extremely rare breed of Yeti. As they were playing, the leader came over and sent Chickendog back.

Elijah Rogers (9)
Stow On The Wold Primary School, Stow On The Wold

The Fluffy Alien Who Has A Bad Enemy

This is the fluffy alien. She is called Bella. She is pink and small. Bella loves to swim every day. She wants to go to the Alien Olympics, but she has a problem.

She has an enemy with four eyes called Jeff. He doesn't want Bella to go to the Alien Olympics because she will be better than him.

So he starts training but he only does it once a day and Bella does it four times a day until Jeff goes up to Bella and says, "Can you teach me, please?"

Bella says, "Sure!"

They both make the Olympics.

Annabelle Wright (9)

Stow On The Wold Primary School, Stow On The Wold

Tyrano-Saurotops

Tyrano-Saurotops is a meat-eating creature that hunts plant eaters. Tyrano-Saurotops was made by a T-rex and an alien. It takes three days to hatch. One day Tyrano-Saurotops escapes when the power turns off! It breaks the bars down. Now it is hunting people and it escapes into the woods. So the military is going to try to capture it. Two hours later the military have found it and are now trying to get it asleep with sleepy darts. The military finally hit the huge creature and are now taking it back to the cage.

Jude Williams (9)
Stow On The Wold Primary School, Stow On The Wold

Bob's Big Adventure

One day on Mars, there was a creature called Bob and he looked like a snake. After years of living on Mars, Bob was fed up with living on one planet. He wanted to see more. So when astronauts came to Mars about 'stuff', Bob jumped on the rocket and, as they came back, he hid in the closet. He saw more of his kind in boxes, not cardboard boxes, test boxes. So Bob quickly grabbed the keys from the high shelf over him and let them go. After that Bob decided he was going to stay on Mars, forever.

Thea Shaw (11)
Stow On The Wold Primary School, Stow On The Wold

Leo The Footballing Monster

Once, there was a footballing monster named Leo. He played day and night, so when he saw a house brimming with footballs; he was ecstatic.

He casually walked over to the house and entered through the door. This was his mistake. He turned and saw something that made him *shiver*; a cat! A few seconds later, he was running for his life! But wait, he wasn't running. *Phew.* "Wait a minute," he said, turning around. "Human!" The small girl named Jenny picked him up and petted him. Although he didn't play football, he thought humans weren't so bad after all.

Rory Babiker (10)
The Oratory Preparatory School, Goring Heath

Untitled

Once there was a mythical monster called the Gloomy-Gobble. He liked going into classrooms to mess around because he could shape-shift into anything and change his voice well.

One day, he went into the maths classroom without any students or teachers looking and then became the answer sheet on one of the students' desks. The student hid it under the desk without anyone looking. Then the Gloomy-Gobble made a sound in a girl's voice, saying, "I'm here."

Then the teacher heard and ripped the sheet out of the student's hand and said, "You're expelled!"

Gabriel Surplice

The Oratory Preparatory School, Goring Heath

The Turbo Twins

"Get out!" yelled Bart. "You don't belong here!"
The Turbo Twins packed and left the only home
they had ever known. They had always been
bullied by another washing machine called
Blundering Bart. So, they set off to a planet with
an odd name, Earth.
Dryer and Washy landed on Earth with a
breathtaking bump. A small girl, Lotta, saw them
crash from her bedroom window. She pulled on her
scarlet dressing gown. Soon, she was standing in
front of them. The twins explained themselves.
They were worried Lotta wouldn't like them, but
she gave them a huge hug!

Catherine O'Sullivan (10)
The Oratory Preparatory School, Goring Heath

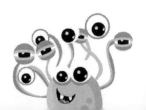

Scaryton The Robot's Story

Scaryton the robot is the scariest of them all. Scaryton the robot likes toys but especially Minecraft. Scaryton the robot can go into people's dreams. Scaryton the robot likes to play with people in their dreams.
But one day, Scaryton the robot saw Wuzardlord Zombie. They didn't like each other because one time, both of them went into the same person's dream and they couldn't use their powers while they were in the same dream. This day, they got in the same dream again and saw each other, but they could use their powers because they became friends.

Grigoril Puzanov (10)
The Oratory Preparatory School, Goring Heath

The Monster Whose Life Got Worse

There was a monster called Alfie who lived in Monster Mania. He wanted to explore the different planets, but disaster had struck! One day, he was walking down the street and was shot with a chemical called 'Disappear If You Dare'. From that day on, he had invisibility powers and could use them whenever he wanted. At school when he was doing work, he turned invisible, and when the teacher wasn't looking he picked up his water bottle and poured it down his teacher's back! When they found out it was him he got expelled and turned to crime.

Arin Ruparelia (10)
The Oratory Preparatory School, Goring Heath

Nachos

Many years ago, there was this planet called QRVI2053X, and on this planet there lived a cyborg snake dragon, called Nachos, and his planet was suffering from a terrible rainstorm because his species was part-robot. They would suffer much more than any other creature on the planet. But Nachos was the smartest of his kind.

Disaster struck! The news said that in five days' time the storm would destroy the planet, so Nachos put together a plan, a plan to make a wall between the land and the sea. It took him four days but he did it!

Grace Morphy (10)
The Oratory Preparatory School, Goring Heath

Scales The Slithery Sea Serpent

A long time ago, on a planet called QRCXVY, there was a mysterious ancient animal called Scales. Scales liked to eat little children and could shape-shift into anything and try to trick children and eat them, but it didn't always succeed.

One day, it was waiting to pounce when Scales noticed a group of children doing handstands and cartwheels in the water. Scales thought that maybe it could shape-shift into a child and do a handstand in the water, so when it shape-shifted into a child and did a handstand, the children were eaten.

Anabella Fowler (9)
The Oratory Preparatory School, Goring Heath

The Devil And The Warlock

The bad people will want to watch out for the Devil and the Warlock because they send people who are mean and bad to Hell. They destroy the soul and the soul will never survive, but people who are good and kind will go to Heaven. Their souls will not get destroyed and they will turn into another human being. The Devil is after a teacher called Miss Trunchbull who treats kids badly, she works with a witch but the Devil works with the Warlock who also came from Hell. Together they are looking for Miss Trunchbull and the witch.

Shubh Puthan (11)
The Oratory Preparatory School, Goring Heath

Timmy The Tickler Strikes Again

One day, Timmy was hiding in the closet, ready to tickle. He has a main enemy and a lot of the time he's in the closet waiting.

His enemy opened the door to the closet, and he was ready to attack. He jumped out and tickled her to death! Timmy snuck downstairs to the living room, and Dad was there. Timmy went behind Dad and tickled him on the neck. Dad laughed so much that he went unconscious. Timmy then made his way to the kitchen. Mum was making breakfast. She noticed him and hit him on the head with a frying pan.

Alexander Rolfe (10)
The Oratory Preparatory School, Goring Heath

Bizzle The Stalker

Once, on a normal, but not-so-normal Monday morning, it was raining in London and a family were sitting on their sofa because they had nothing really to do. They lived in a flat in central London, with two tabby cats. They were in the middle of their movie when they felt something under the sofa but they just thought it was their cats. But it wasn't. It was a little, furry monster called Bizzle, a little, dirty, blue monster under there. He was a mischievous monster who had been following them everywhere they went.

Poppy Howarth (9)
The Oratory Preparatory School, Goring Heath

Granny!

Once, in a dark wood, there lived an old, horrible granny. She had 3 hands and 1 eye because she had been bitten by Billy Biter when she was little. A few months later, Granny had got lots of visitors. A few children had been knocking on Granny's door lately. She was very angry so she took some string and an iron and tied them to her outdoor, scary steps so if anyone tried to bug her again they would get hurt. She looked out of her bedroom window to see people throwing eggs at her windows. She will get revenge!

Georgie Whale (10)
The Oratory Preparatory School, Goring Heath

One-Tailed Fox

Deep in the forest, there was an ancient village of foxes. There was a one-tailed fox. She was the weakest of her village. Soon, the village came hunting for her. As she ran, she stopped at a castle. As she stepped in, a ten-tailed fox, Darkness Fox, came. Because she didn't have any power, she got hurt easily. Then, she saw a dead ten-tailed fox and took his tails. She became an eleven-tailed fox. She became stronger and defeated the ten-tailed fox and returned to her village where no one ever hurt her again.

Laila Sun (9)
The Oratory Preparatory School, Goring Heath

Destiny Awaits!

Once upon a time, in the land of Hope, there lived a monster called Scary Ficklebot. She was having an amazing day. She had just been selected for the two monsters who go down to Earth and disguise themselves as humans to comfort others. The best part was that she was paired up with her super BFF Cackle Mot. Scary was so happy. They finally made it down to Earth and disguised themselves as Sophia and Lucy. They decided to help a girl called Allegra. She felt a lot better. Scary was so grateful for Cackle.

Lily Irving (9)
The Oratory Preparatory School, Goring Heath

The Blob

Do you ever lose your homework and say either the dog ate it or it was a ghost? No. You are wrong. It was a blob. He is a monster that can turn into any liquid. It could be water, it could be melted chocolate - anything at all. He gets into your water bottle at the end of the day and while you are asleep, it creeps out of your water bottle, goes into your backpack and *gobbles up your homework!* And when you wake up, *your homework is gone!* Well, now you have an excuse. It was a blob!

Chloe Conway (10)
The Oratory Preparatory School, Goring Heath

137

Untitled

Once upon a time, there was a monster called Tessa Ticks. She was short, hairy and naughty to others. When she went to the disco she made the disco ball fall to the ground, and then everyone ran out of the disco and Tessa got the disco all to herself. So then, she practised her dance moves. After that, she went back to her house where she saw her best friend from a different world. She was so happy and they had a cup of coffee and went on a big mission to find all the discos in the world.

Miela Glover (9)

The Oratory Preparatory School, Goring Heath

Untitled

In a village far away, a girl whose name was Indigo Glory was born on Halloween night. A pretty girl she was, but she was evil with purple eyes and a thirst for blood. When she had grown up she lived in a cave and ate animals that ate endangered species.

One day, Indigo went to a lake to see if she could catch a feast, but she sprang too early and went splashing into the lake. A secret Indigo kept to herself was that she could not swim, and she drowned, never to be seen again.

Alexandria Johnson Cox (10)
The Oratory Preparatory School, Goring Heath

Untitled

Big Mouth Barry, born as a human, got eaten by a Big Mouth and was now formed as a monster. Everyone was scared of him. He decided to eat buildings, he loves the ones with food in them. But one day he got too fat and he became human once again. He was furious, he still had his big mouth so he ate all the people he could see! Then, a girl called Hope melted his heart. She was kind and they happily walked away together and lived happily ever after, and lived together forever.

Kathryn Jones (9)
The Oratory Preparatory School, Goring Heath

Willow Whisp's Journey

A swooping beast roamed the sky. Whilst flying, it swooped down at the speed of light and landed, looking around. It heard a rustle; so it quickly ran away.

It helped the animals find food and shelter.

Afterwards, it flew to the moon and fell asleep.

When it woke up, it stopped the asteroids in mid-air with its powers!

It flew around the solar system, stopping the asteroids and watching the stars; then went back home.

Willow Whisp fell asleep once again.

Alexandra Cockman-Goodford (10)
The Oratory Preparatory School, Goring Heath

Forky

There once was a fork called Forky. He was once a little boy like anyone in the world. Then, at school, he read a book from the library and he loved it, so he started to become a monster and turned into a massive fork! Everyone was scared because he tried to stab them with his fork.

One day, he met a little boy who loved Forky and kept saying he was cool and asked him to be his friend. Forky was confused but said yes. The boy was kind so Forky became human again.

Lily Jones (9)

The Oratory Preparatory School, Goring Heath

Valcna The Fire Demon

Long as a house, tall as a tree, a snake with purple-black scales, black horns, menacing glowing red eyes and a tail with spikes and fire at the end of it. This monster is called Valcna the Immortal Fire Demon. Many heroes have gone searching for him but always came home with no luck until a boy called Will Zim finally found him and woke him from his slumber. Now, the world may end.

Lilly Pirrie (11)
The Oratory Preparatory School, Goring Heath

Untitled

James woke up in a familiar place, although he couldn't remember. He got up and it was pitch-black, he could not even see five feet ahead. To his knowledge, he felt books so the room must have been a library. He pulled a rusty and stiff lever and a secret compartment opened. He heard low rumbling but nothing was there, he thought it could be his stomach.

Bridget Moorcroft (10)
The Oratory Preparatory School, Goring Heath

144

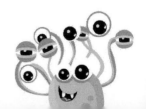

Taking Over The World

One day there was a man, he adopted a dragon lizard. He named him Destroyer. Destroyer had lived with Mohamed for a long time now. Suddenly, one morning, there was a huge thud! They woke up from the loud noise. They looked out of the window and saw other monsters invading Earth. They had to do something about this. Destroyer carried Mohamed to the top of a tree. But their army was enormous. Destroyer couldn't do it alone, so he bit Mohamed and now they both had powers. They demanded the other monsters to stop. But it was too late, they had destroyed the whole city.

Mohamed Fakih (9)
Wilbury Primary School, Edmonton

Powered Out

One morning, a group of creatures were saving the world. Oblater had the most wonderful power - fire breath. The whole group of creatures made fun of him. He wondered why his power was useless. Suddenly their day came, a mission to capture a dragon.

They set off on the quest. They arrived at the cave, they found the dragon and got out their powers. They defeated the dragon. Oblater and the dragon had the same power. They realised his power was the same as the dragon. They immediately apologised to him and they became friends again. They lived happily ever after.

Safiya Shah (8)
Wilbury Primary School, Edmonton

Fupple And Jaleel

Fupple was from a faraway universe. He got lost in space and landed on Earth. Everyone was scared of him, but a friendly boy named Jaleel adopted him. Aliens from an asteroid at the edge of the universe invaded Earth. Fupple shape-shifted to look like one of them and quickly shot out his long, sticky tongue and ate them all as quickly as a snake swallowing a spider! Fupple had saved the world. Jaleel took him to the Prime Minister who gave Fupple a medal and said that he could go to school.

Jaleel McKenzie (8)
Wilbury Primary School, Edmonton

147

Ali And Mostafa

One day, there was a boy and his enthusiastic monster. This monster was called Mostafa, and his strong powerful owner was called Ali. The police had put them in prison! It was because they thought they were bad. Ali and Mostafa both had powers and they used them to help the city, but they thought they were trying to destroy the city, but then they broke out using their laser vision. Then they said, "We are not trying to end the city, we're trying to help it."

Hassan Fakih (9)
Wilbury Primary School, Edmonton